THE MIRACLES OF
JESUS

THE MIRACLES OF
JESUS

Ellyn Sanna

BARBOUR
PUBLISHING

© 2000 by Barbour Publishing, Inc.

Written by Ellyn Sanna. Illustrated by Ken Save.

Print ISBN 978-1-62416-252-7

eBook Editions:
Adobe Digital Edition (.epub) 978-1-62416-399-9
Kindle and MobiPocket Edition (.prc) 978-1-62416-398-2

Cover design: Greg Jackson, Thinkpen Design
Cover illustration: Steve James

Published by Barbour Publishing, Inc., P.O. Box 719, Uhrichsville, Ohio 44683, www.barbourbooks.com

Our mission is to publish and distribute inspirational products offering exceptional value and biblical encouragement to the masses.

 Member of the
Evangelical Christian
Publishers Association

Printed in the United States of America.
Offset Paperback Manufacturers, Dallas, PA 18612; June 2013; D10003979

Contents

Solve the Secret Code!

At the end of each chapter, you'll find a set of numbers—it's the code to a secret message throughout the book.

Each group of four numbers stands for a single letter in the message. Your job is to pinpoint each mystery letter with the codes, then write the letters above each four-digit number group. When you've finished solving each chapter's code, read the letters from chapter one through the end of the book to find out exactly what the secret message says!

Here's how to use the codes:

- The first number is the page number—within that chapter.
- The second number is the paragraph on the page—count full paragraphs only.
- The third number is the word in the appropriate paragraph.
- The fourth number is the letter in the appropriate word—this is the letter you'll write above the number group.

Enjoy the story. . .and solving the secret message!

1
The Kingdom of Heaven

"Come on," Aaron called over his shoulder. "Grandfather John promised to tell me one of his stories. You can listen, too."

Eleven-year-old Rachel hung back, frowning. Aaron was her new friend—her only friend here in Ephesus—and she liked being with him. But listening to an old man talk didn't sound very interesting to her. Besides, she was hungry. She had planned on heading for the market, hoping that someone would have bruised figs they would be willing to give her. And maybe she could even get hold of a bone for soup. That would make her mother happy. . . .

Ever since her father died two years ago, Rachel was nearly always hungry. Her mother did the best she could to find them food, but they had no relatives to help support them, and they grew poorer and poorer. They had moved from Corinth to Ephesus last spring, hoping things would be better, but their house here was little more than a few boards nailed together.

Rachel's eyes burned as she thought about their troubles. *It's not fair,* she thought fiercely.

They hadn't done anything to deserve such a cold, hungry, sad life. She was tired of always thinking about food; she was tired of her mother always being sad and weary; and most of all she was tired of always missing her father. . . .

Aaron broke into her thoughts. "Come on," he insisted. He walked backward down the street, grinning at her. "You'll like Grandfather John. I promise."

Rachel made a face. But when Aaron

ducked through an arched opening in the wall beside the street, she sighed and followed him through into an inner courtyard.

They found an old man sitting on a stone bench, the sun shining on his snow-white hair. He turned his lined face toward the two children and smiled. "Aaron." His dark eyes were bright with welcome. "And who is your friend?" His gaze moved to Rachel's face with gentle curiosity.

Self-consciously, Rachel tucked her hair behind her ears and smoothed her ragged robe, suddenly aware that her face and hands were dusty, and her hair was snarled and rough. Lately, her mother had no time to notice if Rachel was clean or not—and somehow Rachel always forgot to check until it was too late.

"This is Rachel. She's new in Ephesus."

Aaron flung himself down on the dirt at the old man's feet. "Her mother is a widow," he added bluntly.

Rachel felt herself flush, and she wished she and Aaron were alone so she could smack him on the head. She scowled down at her dirty toes. "I should go," she muttered.

The old man put out a thin, wrinkled hand. "No, stay. Please." He met Rachel's eyes and smiled. "My grandson loves to hear stories about the Master. You're welcome to listen, too."

Rachel bit her lip, uncertain whether to go or stay. She had chores to do before her mother came back from "gleaning"—picking up the unwanted loose grain from the farmers' fields outside the city wall. Rachel was still hoping to get something from the market, something to ease the emptiness in her own stomach and a bit more to surprise her mother. But the sun was still high in the sky, and she supposed she could be hungry a little longer. Something about the old man's face made her want to stay, even if she had to listen to boring stories about long ago. She plopped down in the dust beside Aaron and asked, "Who is the Master?"

Aaron nudged her with his elbow. "You know—the Messiah. Jesus the Christ. You've heard my parents call Him the Master."

Rachel shrugged. She usually didn't pay much attention to what grown-ups said, except when they gave her food. Since her father died, Rachel was too busy figuring out how to help her mother get their next meal. Aaron's mother often gave Rachel baskets of bread and cheese, and Rachel was always both grateful and embarrassed. But she had never noticed Aaron's mother talking about any "master."

Aaron was staring at her, his eyebrows raised. "You do know who Jesus is, don't you?"

Rachel shrugged again. She seemed to remember her father once saying something about Jesus of Nazareth. . .and maybe she'd heard some gossip in the marketplace, back when they lived in Corinth. "Wasn't He a magician or something?" The look on Aaron's face made her search her mind for something more. "He was crucified, wasn't He?" She turned away from Aaron's disgusted expression and looked up at the old man.

John nodded gravely. "Yes, He was crucified. But He was more than a magician. He was the Son of God. He *was* God, come down to be with us."

Rachel tucked in the corner of her

mouth. The old man didn't look crazy, but still
. . . "How do you know?" she asked flatly.

Aaron pushed his sandal against Rachel's
ankle. "Grandfather John was one of the Master's twelve disciples," he told her between his
teeth. Aaron was clearly not pleased with Rachel's ignorance. "He spent three years with
Jesus. He *knew* Him better than anyone. They
were friends."

Show some respect, Aaron's brown eyes told
Rachel silently. She looked away from his gaze,
back to the old man. He smiled at her, apparently undisturbed, and put a quieting hand on
his grandson's shoulder.

"Jesus proved to us who He was by signs
and miracles," he told Rachel gently.

"So He *was* a magician," Rachel said stubbornly. "Like I said." She searched her memory
for the gossip she had heard about this man.
"Didn't He claim to be able to turn water into
wine, stuff like that?"

John nodded. "He did turn water into wine
once, at a wedding in Cana. But His miracles
were not just tricks meant to entertain. His
miracles told us about God. They showed us the
kingdom of heaven."

Rachel wrinkled her nose. "Heaven?" she

repeated, not sure what the old man meant. "You mean like when we die?"

"M-m-m." John squinted up at the sky and shook his head. "All this—" He waved his hand around the courtyard, taking in the small square house and the city street beyond the wall. "Ephesus, the lands beyond, they are all part of the Roman emperor's kingdom. Once we Jews lived in the kingdom ruled by David's throne, and we long for the day when  our land will be our own again. But David and the Roman emperors both ruled earthly kingdoms, kingdoms we can see and touch."

He smiled up at the blue sky above his head, and his voice became softer, filled with a strange joy that Rachel did not understand. "But there is another kingdom all around us, an invisible kingdom, the kingdom of heaven. Jesus is the Lord of this realm—and through faith in Him, the things we can see and touch become part of heaven's kingdom. We who follow the Master believe that through faith we are now citizens of heaven. And our Lord's miracles showed us that He controls our world, that He has the power to bring everything under His rule. His miracles showed us who God is—and they showed us what His kingdom is like."

Rachel's eyes followed the old man's gaze to the blue sky. Her stomach growled loudly, distracting her for a moment, but in spite of herself, she was interested in this invisible kingdom. She wondered if people still got hungry once they were citizens of heaven. Then she shook her head at her own thoughts, and her eyes dropped back to the dusty earth beneath her. "It still sounds like magic to me," she said.

"No," John said gently. "It is not magic. Jesus had amazing power, it is true, but He did not use His power to impress people or for His own purposes. His miracles tell us good news—that God's love is with us. God's kingdom is real, even more real than the world we see around us."

Rachel was silent while her mind pondered these new ideas. Beside her, Aaron sat quietly, his chin on his drawn-up knees. She glanced at him, glad he was no longer impatient with her, and then she turned back to John once more. "And you actually saw this Jesus perform these miracles? They weren't tricks?"

"I saw them," John affirmed. "They weren't tricks."

Rachel studied his face, wondering if he spoke the truth. Somehow, his words made her prickle inside. She felt something strange, something different than she had felt since her father died. It felt like. . .hope.

She sniffed. What use would an invisible kingdom be to her mother and her? *It won't feed us,* she reminded herself.

"So tell me about these miracles," she said to the old man. She knew her voice was louder than it should be. *Talk like a woman,* her mother was always reminding her. *Speak softly, with your eyes lowered. You are rude when you look older people full in the face and talk with that sharp little voice of yours.* But speaking softly made Rachel feel angry. Besides, no one noticed a grimy, ragged little girl if she didn't look straight at them and *make* them see her. Rachel lifted her chin a notch, daring the old man to disapprove of her. "What was the greatest miracle Jesus ever did?"

The old man smiled at her with such a look of acceptance and love that Rachel blinked. He sat back on the stone bench more comfortably, and then he closed his eyes and tilted his face toward the sun's warmth. Rachel thought he was going to sleep, but then he said slowly, "I suppose the greatest miracle of the Master's life would have to be the one that started them all."

"You mean the time He turned the water into wine?" Aaron asked.

His grandfather shook his head. "No. That miracle and all the others were caused by this first great miracle—and they all proved that it was true." He fell silent.

"So what was it?" Rachel asked impatiently.

John opened his eyes. "Why, His birth."

Secret Code:

___ ___ ___
3-4-1-2 10-2-6-1 7-2-2-6

___ ___ ___ ___
2-4-2-1 5-1-1-1 1-2-1-6 9-1-6-4

___ ___ ___ ___ ___
8-2-2-2 6-5-5-1 2-1-4-4 3-3-3-5 4-2-1-1

2
The Birth of Jesus

"In the beginning," John began, "before any-thing else existed, Jesus was already alive. We can't imagine what that must have been like, because we can't imagine anything beyond what we have always known. But there in the darkness, before the sun and the stars began to burn, was God, and Jesus was with Him. Jesus wasn't just *with* God, though. He actually *was* God. God the Creator and Jesus and the Holy Spirit are all separate and yet one, the way the three strands of a rope twist together to make one cord.

"Jesus was there when the earth was formed,

and the water, and the sky, and all the living things on the earth. His power was at work while all these things were being made, because nothing exists anywhere that He didn't make. He made life, because He is where all life begins. This life gives light to us all today, and it has lit the lives of the generations of people who have lived upon the earth since our father, Adam and our mother, Eve. Jesus continues to give light and life forever, because nothing can ever blow out His light. In the darkness, before Creation, it shone as brightly as it does now, and it shines the same even in the midst of sadness and hurt and evil. Death itself cannot cast a shadow over the light of Christ.

"And this same Jesus, this ageless, undying Being, *loves* us. Before the world was made, He loved you and me. He loved us so much that He did something amazing, something truly miraculous. He became a human baby and was born to a virgin named Mary.

"Can you imagine what that means? The

Creator of the universe loved us so much that He emptied Himself of all His power. As the Son of God, He could be everywhere at the same time. He could do anything at all, so awesome was His power. And He knew everything, all the secrets of the universe. But He gave up all that and became a tiny, helpless little baby.

"Before He was born, the angels told His parents, Mary and Joseph, what was going to happen. And on the night He was born, heaven's choir sang to some poor shepherds who were watching their sheep out on the hills. A few other people were told of this marvelous thing that was happening.

"But for the most part, Jesus arrived on earth very quietly. He grew up in Nazareth, the Son of God now a simple carpenter. But those who knew Him then already noticed something different about Him. He was so  full of love. Everything about Him reached out to others.

"Most of us, you know, even children, walk

around with walls around our hearts. But Jesus didn't have any walls. He gave Himself to everyone He met. And He didn't try to protect Himself with lies and fancy acts to impress others. No, He always told the truth. His life *was* the truth.

"Now God sent another man, Jesus' cousin, John the Baptist, to tell people that God's Son was coming to change their hearts. John the Baptist was like a big signpost pointing toward Jesus. 'Change the way you live!' John shouted. 'Stop being so selfish! Start loving each other! Start sharing with each other! Someone is coming who is far greater than I am, for He existed long before I did.'

"But even though John did what He could to get people ready for the Messiah, a lot of people still did not recognize Jesus when they saw Him. They had a picture in their heads of what the Messiah ought to act like—they thought He would give them lots of earthly things, things they could see and touch—but Jesus didn't give them any of those things they wanted. And they thought that if Jesus was God, then He ought to keep all the rules—those do's and don't's created by the religious leaders—but instead of following each and every law, Jesus kept breaking them left and right.

"So even though Jesus made the entire world, people didn't recognize who He was. The people in His own town didn't even believe in Him.

"But some of us did open our hearts to Him. And when we broke down the walls around our hearts, when we stopped living as though we each were the very center of the universe, Jesus made us a part of His kingdom. He made us children of God. Inside, we are like new people, as clean and innocent and loving as little babies. That's because you could say that through Jesus we've been 'born again.'

"Jesus' entire life showed us the love of God. That's because Jesus *was* God—God as a little baby. And, of course, then He grew and became a little boy who ran around and played and skinned His knees. He got hungry and He was sad sometimes and He laughed a lot. He was just like you and me. And He was also God. He was never ever

21

selfish, because He was love in human form.

"And *that* is the greatest miracle of all. All the other smaller miracles just helped us see the truth a little more clearly."

Secret Code:

___ ___ ___ ___ ___
5-1-1-1 2-2-3-1 3-1-6-3 1-1-1-2 1-2-7-3

___ ___ ___ ___ ___
6-1-5-5 4-1-4-7 5-2-4-1 2-1-6-4 1-1-7-3

___ ___ ___
2-1-7-3 3-3-7-3 5-3-4-6

3
The Truth

Rachel wrapped her arms around her knees. She had a sudden lonely feeling inside her heart that she didn't understand. The old man's story had been interesting enough, and Aaron was smiling at her now, his eyes bright with friendship. In Corinth, before she and her mother moved to Ephesus, the other children used to throw stones at her sometimes and make fun of her bare feet and ragged robe. Now that Aaron was her friend, no one ever teased her when she went through the market asking for food. So why should she be lonely?

She hunched her shoulders. Maybe it was

just her hungry stomach that made her feel so empty. But she found herself wishing that she could have seen Jesus when He was a baby—or had Him for a friend when He grew older.

He must have had rich parents, she decided, thinking about what the old man had said about Jesus, how He always told the truth and reached out to other people. Only a rich boy could do that. Someone poor like her had to protect herself—and she had to tell lies. How else could she take care of herself and her mother? She squinted her eyes and pushed the lonely feeling away. Why would she want to be friends with a spoiled rich boy?

"What are you thinking?" the old man asked her softly.

She shrugged. "All that stuff you said about Jesus not needing any walls around His heart. I bet He had lots of money, didn't He? Rich people can afford to be nice."

John laughed. "No," he said, "Jesus never

had much money. In fact, His parents were so poor that He was born in a stable with the animals. And when He grew up, He never owned more than His robe and sandals. He didn't even have a home of His own."

Rachel's eyes widened with surprise. At least she and her mother had a place to sleep, even if it was tiny and dark and dirty. She shook her head. "Maybe that's why He didn't have any money then. Because He was too foolish to take care of Himself. People who are too trusting never end up with anything."

She heard Aaron take an indignant breath. "The Master wasn't foolish. He was wise and good and—"

John touched his shoulder gently. "The wisdom of heaven looks like foolishness to those who live only in this world we see and touch."

Rachel pressed her lips together and glared at Aaron. It was easy enough for him to believe in this Jesus—after all, Aaron had a father who was alive and well, and his family had enough money to feed themselves. "I've got to go," she said stiffly. "I need to get to the marketplace. My mother wants me to buy bread and olives for tonight's supper." As she spoke the lie, she raised her head and stared into the old man's face.

He looked back at her, his eyes full of that peculiar love she had noticed earlier. She had the uncomfortable feeling, though, that he saw straight through her lie, and her face burned.

"Are you hungry?" he asked her.

"Not particularly," she said in a cold voice.

"Are you hungry?" he repeated.

She sighed. "I already said I'm not hungry." But her stomach betrayed her and growled loudly again, and she felt her face grow hotter.

The old man's gentle gaze never moved from her face. "I have some bread and cold meat inside that I was going to eat for my lunch. There is plenty there for all three of us." He smiled into Rachel's embarrassed eyes and asked her one more time, "Are you hungry?"

She drew her finger back and forth in the soft earth. "Yes," she said at last.

John looked delighted with her answer. "There," he said softly. "Now I can get you something to eat." He got to his feet and slowly went inside.

While he was gone, Rachel kept her eyes on the lines she was drawing in the dust, but Aaron nudged her with his foot. "Why do you lie like that?" he asked her, his disgust plain in his voice. "It's silly."

"I know," she muttered. It *had* been a silly lie. After all, what she wanted was food, and saying she wasn't hungry wouldn't get her what she wanted. But sometimes she was ashamed to admit to her hunger. She hadn't wanted the old man to know just how poor she and her mother were.

John returned with bowls of food. Rachel and Aaron balanced them on their knees while the old man sat beside them on the bench. Ra-chel tried hard not to wolf the food, but there hadn't been any breakfast that morn-ing, and the rolls were fresh and soft.

When she was fi-nally full, she looked up at the old man. "Thank you," she said gruffly.

"You are welcome," he answered. "Do you understand why I asked you three times if you were hungry?"

She scowled and shook her head.

"Your lies built a tall wall around yourself. You thought you would be safe behind your wall, but you were scared, and so you built your wall higher still." He shook his head. "We are all the same. And the truth is, until we break down our walls, until we dare to speak the truth, God cannot give us the good things He longs for us to have. We are too full of ourselves to have room for His blessings."

Rachel swallowed a last bite of bread. She wiped the crumbs from her mouth with the back of her hand. Now that she wasn't hungry anymore, she didn't feel as trembly inside, and she said loudly, "It's hard to care about all that stuff the priests and rabbis talk about in the synagogue—God's blessings and all that—when you're hungry." *There,* she thought defi-

antly, *if they want me to be honest, I'll be honest.*

"When I spoke of God's blessings," John said mildly, "I was referring to this." He touched a finger to the basket of left-over bread. "Food is certainly one of God's greatest blessings."

Rachel shook her head. Her father had studied the law and the prophets every day, and he had often gone to the synagogue to listen to the rabbis—but he had never once mentioned to his daughter that God cared about something as ordinary as bread. She let out a small, sharp breath of laughter. "You mean eating and drinking is a part of your kingdom of heaven? I thought it was invisible. Do invisible people have to eat and drink?"

John laughed out loud, a delighted creaky chuckle, and even Aaron grinned. Rachel turned red again, afraid that they were laughing at her, but she could not mistake the kindness in the old man's eyes.

"We all can be a part of the Lord's kingdom," he said. "But that does not mean we will become invisible. And it certainly does not mean that we will stop eating and drinking. No, our bodies and all that we see and touch become a part of something bigger, something that means far more. God takes the things of this world and uses them for His kingdom. Eating and drinking were very important to Jesus."

Rachel muttered, "He must have been a jolly fat man."

Aaron kicked her, but John only laughed again. "No, He was not fat. We are not to make eating more important to us than God. But God does expect us to enjoy our food."

"Why would the Creator of the universe care if we like to eat?"

"Because He made us that way. He takes delight in what He has created."

Rachel narrowed her eyes at the old man. "How do you know all this? You sound as though everything you say is absolutely true, when really it's just your opinion." *Rachel,* her mother's voice scolded inside her head, *you're being rude,* but Rachel ignored her mother's warning.

John shook his head. "I know this is true, because I learned it from the Master Himself. And His miracles proved that God cares about food and drink."

"You mean that trick He did when He turned water into wine?"

Aaron let out an impatient sigh. "Grandfather John keeps telling you, Rachel—Jesus didn't do tricks. He wasn't a magician. He was real. Everything He did was true."

John nodded. "Let me tell you about the time the Master turned the water into wine.

And then I will tell you about another time when He fed a crowd of more than five thousand people with just five loaves of bread and two small fishes."

Rachel frowned. "That's impossible."

But John just smiled and began to tell his story.

Secret Code:

__ __ __ __ __
3-3-1-1 5-3-2-3 1-1-4-4 8-1-4-2 6-3-3-1

__ __   __ __ __
2-2-4-6 4-3-1-1   7-4-2-3 9-2-9-1 7-1-1-5

                                    -

__ __ __ __
3-1-5-4 5-4-2-2 5-5-5-2 3-2-1-1

__ __ __ __
2-1-1-2 8-5-1-4 7-1-1-3 6-2-7-3

4

Turning Water into Wine

 "Right after Jesus asked me to be His disciple," John said, "He and some of the rest of us—Peter and Andrew, Philip and Nathanael, and myself—were all invited to attend a wedding outside of Nazareth in Cana. We were friends of the bridegroom, and we were looking forward to having a good time at the wedding party.

"Well, the wedding itself went just fine, and we were enjoying ourselves at the reception afterward, when all of a sudden people started whispering. 'Did you hear?' They were saying to each other, 'Can you imagine? They've run out of wine.'

"Everyone was laughing and gasping, and the poor bridegroom was bright red with embarrassment. After all, the bridegroom and his family are expected to provide a big party for everyone after a wedding. 'Do you suppose they're having money problems?' some people were whispering behind their hands.

" 'No,' said others. 'I hear they have plenty of gold. They're just too stingy to buy enough wine for all their guests. How selfish!'

"By this time, the bridegroom had turned redder still, his father was purple, and his mother was as white as her robe. The bride looked like she might begin to cry at any moment.

"Peter and I turned to the Master, wondering what He would say. We knew Him well enough already to know that He wouldn't want people to be ruining the wedding celebration with their whispers and laughter. We were expecting Him to stand up and say something, maybe even scold the people nearest to Him who were busy gossiping.

"Right about then, though, Jesus' mother came hurrying up to Him, telling Him the whole story. We'd always seen how loving and respectful Jesus was to His mother, but now He just looked at her with a funny expression on His face.

" 'Woman,' He said, 'is that really any of our business?'

"At first, He seemed to be scolding her for

being a part of all the gossip, though Mary wasn't really a gossipy sort of woman. But then He said, 'My time has not yet come.'

"At the time, I wasn't sure what He meant. But looking back now, I think He was reminding His mother that He always acted according to the kingdom of heaven's time frame rather than this world's schedule. I've noticed since then that we often think things should happen in a certain way at a certain time—but the kingdom's timing happens differently than we expect.

"Anyway, His mother seemed to understand what He meant. She gave Him a smile, and then she turned to the servants who were dishing out the food. 'Do whatever He tells you to do,' she told them softly.

"They gave her a strange look and kept right on with what they were doing. Peter and I and the rest of us went back to our food, resigned to the fact that there wouldn't be any more wine. And then Jesus got to His feet and walked over to the wall of the courtyard where six stone jars were standing in a row.

"He stood there for a moment looking at those jars, studying them, with an odd sort of smile on His face. He looked as though He might laugh right out loud, though I couldn't see anything particularly funny about those jars. They were those big tall ones that hold twenty or thirty gallons, and we'd all washed our hands in that water before we ate, the way the law requires that we do. So now they had been pushed out of the way along the wall and were standing there empty.

"Jesus motioned to the servants, who by now had finished serving the meal. 'Fill the jars with water,' He told them.

"They gave Him a surprised look, because

35

after all, there really wasn't much point in anyone washing their hands in the middle of a meal. Some of them knew Mary, so they turned to her, and she kind of waved her hand at them, telling them again to do whatever her Son told them to do. So finally, they shrugged their shoulders and filled the jars up to the brim with water.

"We were all expecting that Jesus would want us to wash our hands now, so we put down our meat and the fruits we were eating, and we wiped our greasy hands on our napkins. I suppose we thought that Jesus wanted to talk to us about getting our hearts clean—especially after all the unkind words that had been said about the bridegroom—and we figured that washing our hands again was Jesus' way of showing us what He meant. Or maybe we even thought that He wanted us to stop the celebration altogether.

"But Jesus took us totally by surprise. He pointed to one of the jars of water and said,

'Pour out some now and take it to the master of ceremonies.'

"The servants raised their eyebrows at this, but Mary motioned to them again, and so they did what Jesus asked. And then those of us who were closest noticed something very strange about the water that came out of the jar. We had seen it go in looking just like everyday water, clear and ordinary. But now it looked darker somehow, and thicker. And it smelled like. . . well, it smelled like wine.

"We all got very quiet, and we watched while the servant carried a cup to the master of ceremonies. He was whispering busily to the bridegroom's father, and he looked impatient from being interrupted, but he took a sip from the cup. And then his face lit up.

" 'This is wonder-  ful!' he cried. He called to the bridegroom to come over and then he slapped his friend on the back. 'Usually a host serves the best wine first. Then, when everyone is full and doesn't care, he

37

brings out the less expensive wine. You had us thinking the wine was all gone. But you were simply saving the best wine until now!'

"And that was the first miracle Jesus ever performed. It was the first sign He gave us of what the kingdom of heaven is really like—a place of bounty and richness, a place where there is plenty of God's best for everyone."

Secret Code:

_____ _____   _____ _____ _____
2-5-5-2 4-3-4-1   1-1-1-4 7-1-6-2 5-1-6-5

                                               -

_____ _____ _____ _____ _____
6-3-3-4 2-5-3-1 3-3-4-1 3-3-7-2 7-1-5-2

_____ _____ _____ _____,
5-1-4-3 4-2-6-1 1-1-2-4 2-5-7-3

5
Feeding the Five Thousand

John paused for a moment, allowing his words to sink into his young listeners. Then he began another story:

"After the other disciples and I had been following Jesus for quite some time, one spring morning Jesus suggested that we try to get away from the crowds of people for a while. We could tell He was tired, and we all were looking forward to having some time to relax. So we set off in our fishing boat for the far side of the Sea of Galilee, and then we all sat down together on the hillside. The sun was shining, the grass was fresh and green, and the wind off the sea was warm and soft against our faces. We lay back in the sunshine, happy just to be there with the Master.

"But just as we were settling down, Jesus pointed to the shore. Wouldn't you know it, the people had gotten wind of where we were heading, and they had followed us there. Peter and Andrew moaned and rolled their eyes when they saw that there would be no escaping the crowd, at least not that day. Jesus didn't speak a word of complaint, though.

"But He did turn to Philip and ask, 'How will we feed all these people?' The way He said it wasn't like He was grumbling or like He thought there was no good answer to the question. He sounded like He really wanted Philip to tell Him, but looking back, I suspect He already knew what He was going to do; He was just testing Philip.

"Well, Philip shrugged his shoulders, because he didn't see any possible answer to Jesus' question. He looked out at the size of the crowd that was headed our way, and he sighed. 'There must be five thousand families out there. Even if we had two hundred denarii— and we don't—we still wouldn't have enough to give each person even a bite of bread.' He sounded a little exasperated that Jesus even asked the question.

"Meanwhile, though, Andrew had been moving around in the crowd, talking to the people, and now he came back and dropped down at Jesus' feet. 'There's a boy here who has five barley loaves and two fishes,' he said.

"Some of us laughed out loud, and some of us just looked at him, wondering why he was being so silly to even tell us about such a small amount of food. Andrew spread out his hands. 'I know, I know. That's nothing among so many people. I just thought I'd mention it.'

"But Jesus got to His feet, and He looked as though He thought the problem had been solved. 'Bring the boy to Me,' He said.

"Andrew led the boy through the crowd, and Jesus knelt down beside him. 'I hear you brought a lunch today,' He said to the boy.

"The boy nodded, looking shy. He held out the basket of food for Jesus to see.

" 'That's a good-looking lunch,' Jesus said.

'May I have it?'

"The boy hesitated for just a second. He looked down at his food, and you could tell he had been looking forward to eating it. Then he nodded and silently put the basket in Jesus' hands. Jesus smiled at him.

" 'Thank you,' He said, and then He turned to us. 'Tell the people to have a seat on the grass. They might as well be comfortable while they eat.'

"When everyone was sitting down, Jesus said a blessing over that tiny basket of food, thanking God for what He had given to us through the boy. The crowd was completely silent, watching Him, wondering what He was doing. He began to break the bread into pieces, and you could hear people start to whisper. They must have wondered if Jesus had lost His mind.

"But then He started passing the bread out to the people—and this was amazing—there was enough for everyone there, every father, every mother, every child! When each person had some bread, Jesus turned to the fish and did the same thing. And again, as He passed the fish out, there was plenty for every person there. Not just a bite, or a little snack to tide them over until they could go home and get something better to eat—no, the people all ate until they were full. You should have seen how excited that little boy was when he realized his lunch had fed so many people!

"When everyone had had enough, Jesus turned to us, and with a voice filled with laughter, He said, 'Collect the leftovers now. We don't want to waste anything.'

"So we did, and we each came back with a basket full of food, enough for us all to have a lunch of our own.

"You should have heard the crowd buzzing. 'This must be a prophet that has come into the world,' they were saying—and then they went even further and started talking about crowning Jesus king. But Jesus slipped off into the hills by Himself.

"Well, the other disciples and I waited all afternoon for Him to come back, but as night began to fall we could see a storm was coming up, and we wanted to get the boat back in port. At last we left without Him, figuring He wanted some time to be alone, the way He did sometimes. We rowed about three or four miles, with the wind growing stronger all the time, and we were beginning to think we would never get across the sea. It was really frightening.

"Just then we looked out across the waves and we saw the strangest thing. Someone was walking on the water, coming steadily toward us, stepping over those waves as though they were as solid as earth! Goose bumps popped up on my arms, and I could see Andrew's hair

literally stand on end.

"And then we heard a familiar voice calling to us through the noise of the storm. 'It's Me. Don't be scared.'

"As soon as I heard that voice, I stopped being afraid, but I was still overwhelmed with awe. By that time, I'd seen Jesus do plenty of marvelous things—but nothing as strange as walking on water. I knew then that Jesus was more than just a teacher, more than a prophet even. He really was the Creator Himself, the Son of God.

"Well, we pulled Him up into the boat, and another weird thing happened then; instantly, as soon as He was in the boat with us, we reached the dock we'd been struggling toward. It was like we simply slipped through space all of a sudden and there we were.

"By then, we were all too tired to ask any questions; we just fell asleep on the boat. But when morning came, the crowd caught up with us again. They had seen that Jesus had not left with us the night before, so they couldn't figure out how He had gotten there.

"He didn't answer their questions, though. Instead, He said to them, 'You don't really care how I got here. And all My miracles aren't really the thing that interests you most. You're following Me because I satisfied your hunger yesterday. Don't search for the sort of food that will spoil, but seek the food that lasts forever, the food of eternal life.'

"By this time, we had all seen so many

strange things, that it wouldn't have seemed any stranger to us if Jesus had produced some magical, marvelous source of food that would never rot, that would last forever. So someone asked Him, 'Can You prove that You can do what You're telling us?' And someone else said, 'Moses fed our ancestors manna from heaven. Are You going to give us something like that?' And yet another person asked, 'How can we work for this food? What should we do?'

"Jesus looked out at the faces in the crowd for a moment, as though He were thinking of the right words to make them comprehend. Then He sighed and shook His head, as though He knew we still weren't really ready to understand Him. 'The truth is,' He said quietly, 'what Moses did was not all that important. God gives you the real bread from heaven. The bread that God gives comes down from heaven and gives life to the world.'

"At that, everyone started shouting out, 'Sir, please, give us this bread that You're talking about! We want it now and for always. That way we could feed our families. None of us would ever be hungry again.'

"Jesus just smiled. '*I* am the bread of life,' He said. 'Whoever comes to Me will never be hungry again, and whoever believes in Me will never be thirsty again. Everything that my Father gives to Me, I will pass along to you, and I will never turn anyone away. I have come down from heaven, not to do what I want to do, but to do what My Father wants Me to do. And what He wants is to give you all eternal life.'

"At this, the Jewish leaders in the crowd began to mutter, 'Just who does He think He is, saying He came down from heaven? After all, we know His mother and father. He's Joseph and Mary's son. What is all this talk about magical bread from heaven?'

"Jesus was still smiling, but He shook His head now. 'The only way you are ever going to know God is through Me. I'm not talking about the sort of miracle that Moses did when he gave you manna in the desert, and I'm not talking about the sort of bread that we eat every day. That kind of bread only satisfies your hunger for a little while, and in the end you'll still die. I'm speaking of a different sort of bread altogether, a bread that will make you live forever. I am that bread. The bread that I give you is Myself, My body. I give it away to be the life for the whole world.'

"By this time, as you can imagine, we were all pretty confused. We'd seen Jesus give us real, actual bread, the kind you can sink your teeth into, the kind that fills your stomach. But He was talking about another kind of bread, a bread that was just as real, maybe more so.

"One thing we did know, though. Just like Jesus had made that little boy's bread be enough for everyone, we knew there also would be plenty of this eternal bread He was talking about. No one would be left out, and all could help themselves. All they had to do was come to Jesus—and He would feed them Himself. Then they would live forever."

Secret Code:

___ ___ ___ ___ ___
4-3-1-1 9-2-6-1 6-1-6-1 1-2-4-4 2-2-2-1

___ ___ ___   ___ ___ ___
4-2-1-3 5-1-2-4 7-4-4-2   10-1-6-3 8-2-5-3 6-1-2-1

6

A New Point of View

Rachel shook her head. "Well, I'm still confused. What was He talking about when He said He was bread and people had to eat Him? It sounds pretty weird to me."

John let out a breath of laughter. "We felt the same way at the time. Some of Jesus' followers came right out and said, 'This is more than we can swallow. Why are we even bothering to listen to such silly talk?' "

"So what did Jesus tell them?" Rachel asked. She was surprised to discover she really wanted to know; she was growing more and more interested in this strange man, Jesus of Nazareth.

John looked down into her face. What he saw there seemed to please him, for he smiled as he said, "Jesus asked us, 'So this shocks you, does it? What if one day you see Me going back to the place where I came from? Will you finally understand then?' He sort of sighed and then He tried again  to explain to us. He wasn't talking about earthly food, you see, not the sort of thing you and I and Aaron just ate together. Real food, eternal food, is the sort that belongs to the kingdom of heaven, the invisible world of the spirit. That world is tied to this one—that's why Jesus used that little boy's bread and fish, because He was showing us that He can use any of the things we see and touch, no matter how small they seem to us. But the kingdom of heaven goes far beyond this world. It's more real than anything you can see or touch, and it lasts forever. And when we give everything we have in this world, then Jesus uses it for His kingdom— and He gives us Himself in return. And then our hearts are never hungry again."

Rachel scowled down at her dirty toes, trying hard to understand. She could almost catch a glimmer of what John was talking about, but just as she thought she had it, it slipped away, leaving her frustrated. "It doesn't make sense," she burst out.

"No," John agreed, "it doesn't. Not when you look at it from one point of view. But from another point of view—the kingdom's viewpoint—it makes perfect sense."

"But what good does it do me?" Rachel cried, her cheeks bright red. "What good will Jesus do my mother and me? We'll still be hungry and poor."

John nodded gravely. "Yes, you may be, though that is not what God wants for His people. But in this world, we do suffer. We get hungry and sick. We even die. But when your heart belongs to Jesus and His kingdom, you begin to look at all those things differently."

Rachel drew her toes back and forth in the dust. "My father got sick and died," she muttered. "How am I supposed to look at that any differently?"

Aaron leaned forward and touched Rachel's arm. "Maybe it helps if you keep remembering that this world isn't the end," he said, his voice sounding gruff and shy. "In the kingdom of heaven God wants us all to be whole and healthy." He glanced at his grandfather. "Isn't that right, Grandfather John?"

The old man nodded. "One day in God's kingdom we will all be completely well, completely healthy, exactly the way God wants us to be."

Rachel blinked tears out of her eyes and raised her chin high. "How do you know?" she asked bitterly. "Oh, it sounds good. It's what we'd all like to believe, isn't it? But how do you *know*?"

John spread his hands out. "I know because the Master told me. He showed me with His miracles."

Rachel turned her head and looked at the old man. "So now you're going to tell me that Jesus could make sick people healthy?"

John nodded. "Yes, He could. He did so many times. Let me tell you about three of the people whom Jesus made well."

Secret Code:

$$\overline{\text{1-1-5-1}} \quad \overline{\text{4-2-3-4}} \quad \overline{\text{3-5-8-1}} \quad \overline{\text{2-1-4-3}} \quad \overline{\text{1-3-5-1}} \quad \overline{\text{3-1-5-2}} \quad \overline{\text{4-3-4-3}}$$

7
Miracles of Healing

John clasped his hands behind his head, and began his story:

"We had been traveling around Judea quite a bit, Jesus and the twelve of us, when Jesus decided to go back to Galilee to see His mother and the rest of His family. While we were there, we visited Cana again, the same town where Jesus had turned the water into wine.

"A royal officer happened to be in Cana on business while we were there. This man was in a hurry to get back home, because his little boy was very sick. But when the officer heard that Jesus was in town, he came to Him and said,

'Please, come home with me to Capernaum. My little boy is there, and when I left him he was so sick that I'm afraid he may not live much longer. Please. . .please hurry. Come home with me and cure him.' His voice was choked with tears. 'He's just a little boy. . .and we love him so much. Please come with me and make him well again.'

"This wasn't the first time Jesus had healed someone, you see, and by this time He had quite a reputation. We were always being crowded with sick people who stretched out their hands to Jesus, trying to get close to Him, trying just to touch Him. There was something wonderful about Him, something that flowed out of Him, that made everyone well again.

"But this time Jesus looked at the man for a long time, and then He shook His head. 'I'm not a magician. Why won't you believe in Me without Me doing a work of power?'

"You see, I suppose that royal officer was like a lot of us: He wanted Jesus to do something *for* him. He didn't want to just follow Jesus, no matter what happened, even if his son died.

"Well, Jesus kept on looking into the man's face. His eyes were stern at first, but then they softened. 'Go on home,' He said gently to the officer. 'I don't need to come with you. Your son will live.'

"The man took a deep breath, as though a heavy load had dropped off his shoulders, and a look of joy spread across his face. 'Thank You, Lord,' he whispered, and then he hurried away.

"We all wondered what had happened, so when I bumped into that officer a few weeks later, I asked him how his son was.

"He gave me a big smile. 'He's fine, just fine. As good as new. The Lord healed him.'

"And then he told me what had happened. After he left Cana, when he was still a ways off from Capernaum, he saw two of his servants riding out to meet him. His heart sank, for he was afraid they had been sent to call him home for his son's funeral. But when they got close enough that he could see their faces, he saw they were smiling.

" 'Your boy is going to live!' they shouted to him. 'The fever has broken, and he is sitting up and eating food.'

"Tears of joy rolled down the man's face. 'When did he begin to recover?' he asked them.

" 'It was the strangest thing,' they told him. 'Yesterday morning we thought the boy wouldn't live through the day. And then at one in the afternoon, the fever suddenly left him.'

"The man thought back, and he realized that one in the afternoon was the exact moment when Jesus had told him that his son would live. He hurried home to see his son, and he and his whole family and all of his servants believed in Jesus from that day on.

"Another time when we were in Galilee, we stopped at Capernaum. The royal officer was delighted to see Jesus again, and news that the Master was in town spread pretty quickly. Before long, the house where we were staying was so packed with people that you couldn't have squeezed in even one more skinny child. There was just a little space in the middle of the room, around where Jesus was standing, so He just had room enough to take a breath while He spoke.

"I was packed in with the rest, with someone's

elbow in my back and my toes squashed by the old man next to me. The Master was preaching, and I was listening, when all of a sudden a funny noise above my head made me lose track of what He was saying. It was a scratchy, scraping sort of noise, and all I could think was that a rat was up there, crawling around in the rafters.

"I turned back to Jesus and tried to concentrate—but the next thing I knew, bits of something were falling on my head. Everyone was looking up at the ceiling now, and the Master stopped talking. When I glanced at Him, I saw He was  looking up, too, with an expression of amusement and welcome on His face.

" 'What's happening?' Peter muttered in my ear. But, of course, I didn't know any more than he did.

"Chunks of clay were dropping down on the floor from the ceiling, and people were jumping out of the way. Now there was a hole up there big enough for us to see the sky. And then the hole got bigger yet, a long rectangle large enough that four men could lower another man down through to the space on the floor in front of Jesus.

"You see, these four men had tried to bring their friend to the Master for healing. Their friend had done plenty of bad things in his day, but they loved him anyway, and now that he was paralyzed, they helped take care of him. When they found that the house was too jam-packed for them to bring their friend to Jesus, they didn't let that stop them. No, they just carried their friend up on the roof and dug a hole through the clay bricks.

"Jesus bent over the paralyzed man. 'My son,' He said, 'Your sins are forgiven.'

"There were some religious leaders in the house that day, and I heard them hiss when Jesus said this. 'What?' they muttered to each other. 'He's blaspheming. God is the only one who can forgive sins.'

"Jesus must have heard what they were saying, because He turned to them and said, 'Why are you so upset about what I just said? Do you think it is easier for Me to say to this man, "Your sins are forgiven"?—or "Get up, pick up your mat, and walk"?' Jesus shook His head, looking like He didn't know whether to laugh or let out a big sigh of exasperation. 'All right,' He said at last. 'Let Me prove to you that I, the Son of man, truly do have the authority here on Earth to forgive sins.' He turned back

to the paralyzed man on the floor and bent down to him. 'Stand up, son,' Jesus said softly. 'Pick up your mat and go on home. You're healed.'

"The man just stared up at Jesus for a moment, a stunned look on his face, and then he leapt to his feet with a cry of joy. The crowd around him stood frozen as he pushed his way through. The last we heard of him, he was laughing and calling out the good news to his friends.

"The rest of us began to shout and praise God. 'I've never seen anything like this ever before!' the old man next to me exclaimed.

"I nodded my head. By that time, I had seen Jesus heal plenty of people—but I could never get over the wonder of it. Each time I was filled with awe, and each time I found myself loving my Master even more than I had before.

"A little while after that, we all went up to Jerusalem for one of the Jewish festivals. While we were there, we went by the Sheep Pool, the place they call Bethesda. The story goes that an angel comes down every now and then and stirs up the water, and afterward the first person to jump into the pool will be healed of whatever diseases he or she might have—so sick people all would go there to be healed. The day we happened by was no different. Sick people were lying all over the ground, people who were blind or couldn't walk or were paralyzed. Their families brought them there, and then waited with them in case a miracle would happen in the water.

"The twelve of us were going to go on by, but Jesus walked right into that crowd of sick people. He squatted next to a man who was lying on a blanket beside his crutch, and Jesus began to talk to him. It turned out that this man had been crippled for thirty-eight years.

" 'Do you want to be healed?' Jesus asked him.

"The man shrugged. 'Of course I do. But I

don't have any family to help me get into the pool. While I'm hobbling along with this,' he made a face at his crutch, 'someone else always gets ahead of me.'

"Jesus got to His feet, and then He held His hand out to the man. 'Come on. Leave your crutch there—you don't need it anymore. Just get to your feet, pick up your blanket—and let's go.'

"The man looked up at Jesus for just a second, and then he broke into a grin. Just like that, he jumped to his feet. He was completely healed.

"Later, Jesus talked to the man in the temple. 'Now that you are well,' He told him, 'stop living just for yourself. If you don't change the way you live, you may end up even sicker than you were before.'

"You see, Jesus was trying to show the man that our bodies' sicknesses really don't matter all that much. It's what is in our hearts that is really important.

"Now, this last miracle took place on the

Sabbath, and that made the Jewish leaders angry with Jesus. They said He was disobeying the law, you see, by doing work on the Sabbath.

"But Jesus told them, 'My Father is always working in His creation, and I am working, too.'

"Of course, this just made the Jewish leaders that much angrier with Him, because now Jesus was not only breaking the Sabbath, He was also claiming that God was His Father. But Jesus only gave them a little smile and said, 'I am simply doing what God does. His love works through Me. God gives life, and so do I. If you believe what I'm saying, then you don't have to wait for eternal life—you have already gotten hold of it and it's yours. Nothing I do is selfish, nothing I do is about Me—everything I do is done from love, and that is the message I bring you. That is what Moses was trying to tell you in the first place, when he gave you the Law. But you don't believe Moses, so how can you believe what I'm trying to tell you now?'

"Those Jewish leaders obviously didn't have a clue what He was talking about. They just turned away, their faces hard and angry, and they began to plot how they could get rid of Jesus.

"But the rest of us thought a lot about what

Jesus had said. And as we watched Him heal person after person, we started to understand that Jesus wanted to heal not only our bodies, but our hearts. He wanted to make us whole on the inside, too. He wanted to teach us how to love."

Secret Code:

___ ___ ___ ___ ___ ___
10-1-7-1 1-1-1-4   3-2-1-1 4-2-5-2 6-1-7-3 7-1-3-3

___ ___ ___ ___ :
4-3-4-1 8-1-10-2 10-4-4-1 9-3-3-4

___ ___ ___
1-3-6-1 3-2-8-4 5-1-2-1

___ ___ ___ ___ ___
6-3-1-1 9-2-1-2 10-4-3-2 2-1-1-4 6-1-7-4

8
True Love

Rachel twisted a corner of her robe between her fingers as she thought about the stories John had told. "I already know how to love," she said at last.

"Do you?" John asked.

She glanced at him. "Of course I do. I love my mother."

"That is a start," the old man said gently. "A very good start. But does love control your life? Do you lay down your life for your mother?"

"Of course I—" Rachel shut her mouth in the middle of her sentence, for she suddenly remembered the night before when she had shouted at her mother and refused to sweep the floor. *But that doesn't mean I wouldn't die for my mother,* she told herself, *not if she had to.* Little things like sweeping the floor weren't that important. *Or are they?* she wondered, looking at John's lined face.

"And what about the people in the marketplace?" the old man prodded. "Do you love them?"

Rachel thought of the faces of the vendors at the market. They were kinder to her now that Aaron was her friend, but she still remembered the way they had looked at her when she had first moved to Ephesus. "Get away, you dirty brat!" one woman had shouted at her when Rachel had asked her for some food. Rachel had been very hungry that day, and her mother had been sick; Rachel had next tried to steal some grapes, and a man had chased her and hit her so hard across the head that her ears had rung.

"No," Rachel said between her teeth. "I don't love them. Why should I? They don't love me."

John nodded. "You see, you don't know how to love yet. True love lays itself down, every day, in the smallest and the biggest ways. True love gives and never steals, no matter what. That is the sort of love that Jesus teaches. That is the sort of love He brought to us. That is what He was showing us as He healed the sick when He was here on Earth."

Rachel shook her head. She was thinking

 about her father, remembering the long year before he died. "When my father was sick, my mother went to the temple every day and prayed that he would get better. And then one day, he *was* better. For three whole months we thought the disease was gone. My mother and father praised God. We were so happy. . . ." Rachel blinked her eyes, remembering. "But then he got sick again. And this time he didn't get better, no matter how hard we prayed. This time he died." She looked up at the old man. "Those people that Jesus healed—did they stay healed?"

John nodded. "Yes, I believe they did. But, child, that doesn't mean that eventually they won't die. They weren't given new bodies. By now the officer's boy has grown older, and one day he will die. And the paralyzed man and the man who was a cripple will also die sooner or later, if they have not died already. That is the way these earthly bodies of ours are made."

Rachel's fingers curled into fists. "So what good did it do? What was the point of Jesus healing them when in the end they'll just die anyway? You keep talking about people living forever, but I don't see that happening anywhere. Even Jesus got killed in the end. And look at you—you were one of His best friends, but you're an old man and—"

Aaron kicked her, and she broke off, but John only smiled. "Yes, I, too, will die before too long. I will hate to leave the people I love," he said as he touched Aaron's shoulder, "but I am looking forward to life in the world to come. I know that my Master is the Lord of both life and death, and nothing can ever separate me from His love."

The hungry, empty feeling inside Rachel's heart was back again, but she tried to pretend she felt nothing but impatience. "You can't know that for sure," she spit out. "Your Master may have turned water into wine and fed people and even healed people, but you can't tell me He made anyone live forever."

"No," John said, "not in the way you mean. But He did bring someone back to life."

Secret Code:

$$\overline{\text{4-3-6-2}} \quad \overline{\text{1-1-1-1}} \quad \overline{\text{3-2-5-5}}$$

$$\overline{\text{5-1-7-1}} \quad \overline{\text{1-4-4-4}} \quad \overline{\text{3-2-4-1}} \quad \overline{\text{4-1-4-3}} \quad \overline{\text{5-1-6-1}} \quad \overline{\text{2-2-1-5}} \quad \overline{\text{2-4-2-1}},$$

$$\overline{\text{3-2-8-3}} \quad \overline{\text{4-3-2-1}} \quad \overline{\text{1-1-1-2}} \quad \overline{\text{2-2-2-7}}$$

9

The Raising of Lazarus

Before Rachel could protest, John started his story.

"One of the Master's good friends was a man named Lazarus. Lazarus lived with his two sisters, Mary and Martha, in Bethany, and many times we would go to their house for a time of rest and fun. But one day we got a message from Mary and Martha

that their brother was very sick.

"We were all upset and worried to hear the bad news, but Jesus said to us, 'This sickness that Lazarus has won't end in death. No, the reason for him getting sick has to do with God's glory. God wants to show people what He is really like.'

"So we didn't leave for Bethany the way we had thought we might when we got the news. Instead, we stayed where we were until a couple of days later when Jesus suddenly announced, 'Let's go back to Judea now.'

"We disciples weren't so sure that was a good idea. After all, the last time we'd been in Judea, the Jewish leaders had tried to kill Jesus. But when we suggested to Jesus that maybe this wasn't such a smart time for making a trip, He said, 'Our friend Lazarus has fallen asleep. I need to go and wake him up.'

"That explained why Jesus suddenly wanted to go to Judea, because Bethany was in Judea after all, but it seemed a little silly to us. After all, we hadn't made the trip when we first heard Lazarus was sick, so we couldn't see why we should go now. We all exchanged glances, and then one of us said, 'But, Master, if he's been sick, then sleeping will do him good. If he's resting comfortably, it probably means he's getting over his sickness. We can visit him later when he's all better.'

"But Jesus shook His head, and then He stopped talking in riddles and told us, 'Lazarus is dead. For your sakes, I'm glad I wasn't there, because this will give you another chance to understand who I really am. Come on, now. Let's go see Lazarus.'

"Well, we disciples just looked at each other again. Jesus was always throwing us off balance like that, saying and doing things that seemed to make no sense. And we really were scared to have Jesus go back to Judea where He had so many enemies.

"After a moment, though, Thomas shrugged his shoulders. 'Come on then,' he said and sighed. 'We might as well go with Him. If we have to, we can die with Him, but let's go.'

"So we did. We went to Judea, and we managed to avoid running into any of the Jewish leaders. But when we reached Bethany, we found out that Lazarus had been dead for four days. The place was crowded with people who had come to pay their respects to Mary and Martha.

"Martha must have gotten word from

someone that Jesus was on His way, because she came out to meet us while we were still on the edge of town. When Jesus saw her coming toward Him, He stopped walking and just looked at her. She looked right back at Him, her face all wet with tears. 'Master,' she said, 'if You had only been here, my brother wouldn't have died. I know that God will do whatever You ask.'

"Jesus reached out and touched her face. 'Your brother will live again,' He said gently.

"Martha sniffed back her tears. 'Yes. I know. We will all live again on resurrection day.' But you could tell she was just repeating the words she had heard all her life in the synagogue; she didn't really know what those words meant, and they weren't much comfort to her right then.

"Jesus smiled. 'I am the resurrection and the life. Those who believe in Me, even though they die like everyone else, will live again. Because they follow Me, they will live forever, and they will never truly die. Do you believe this, Martha?'

"She nodded. 'I have always believed You are the Messiah, the Son of God, the one who has come into the world from God.'

"Jesus gave her a hug. 'I'm glad you believe, Martha.' He looked into her face for a moment, and you could see He was pleased with what He saw there. Then He gave her a little push. 'Go get your sister for Me. I need to talk to her as well.'

"So Martha went to get Mary, and Jesus waited for her there on the road. Pretty soon we saw Mary coming toward us, followed by a crowd of mourners. Everyone was sobbing out loud and wailing, and Mary's face was  blotched and swollen with tears. She threw herself at Jesus' feet, not seeming to care that she was getting her face and hands all dirty.

" 'Lord,' she blurted, 'if You had been here, my brother wouldn't have died.' She was sobbing too hard to say anything more.

"As Jesus looked down at her, His expression became troubled. 'Where have you put him?' he asked Mary, and we all heard the catch in His voice.

"She pulled herself to her feet, but she was still crying too much to talk. 'Come and see,' one of her relatives said to the Master.

"As we followed the crowd toward Lazarus's grave, we were feeling pretty sad. Lazarus had been a good friend to us all, and it didn't seem possible that he wouldn't be coming out to greet us soon. Tears were rolling down our own faces, and when I looked over at Jesus, I saw that He was crying, too.

"I knew how much Jesus had loved Lazarus, so I guess I wasn't surprised, but the crowd all started nudging each other and pointing at Jesus' face, murmuring to themselves. Mostly they were sympathetic of Jesus' grief, but I heard someone say, 'This man healed everyone else. Why couldn't He keep His own friend from dying?'

"By this time we reached the cave where they had put Lazarus's body, and I could see that Jesus was really upset. He wiped His hand across His eyes, though, and straightened His shoulders. 'Roll the stone away from the grave's opening,' He called out.

"Like I said, sometimes the things the Master did or said just didn't make much sense. We all just stared at Him. Martha had joined us again, though, and she put her hands on her hips and shook her head. 'Why would You want to open that grave, Lord? By now the smell will be terrible. After all, he's been dead four days now, and the weather's been hot.'

"Martha was always a practical one; she believed in telling things like they were. The Master smiled at her through His tears. 'Didn't I always say that if you really believe, you will see God's glory?'

"Martha stared back at Him for a second, and then she waved her hands at the crowd. 'Go ahead,' she said. 'You heard Him. Roll the stone away.'

"So they did, and everyone stood there as still as can be, wondering what would happen next. Mary had stopped crying and was looking at Jesus with an expression of wonder and relief, but Martha's face was perfectly blank, as though she were afraid to hope.

"Jesus looked up at the sky and began to pray out loud. 'Father,' He said, 'thank You for hearing Me. Of course You and I both know

that You always hear me, but I'm saying it out loud for the benefit of this crowd of people standing here listening. I want them to see that You really did send Me to them.'

"Jesus' tears had disappeared now, and His face was shining with joy. He took a step toward the grave and leaned in the dark hole. 'Lazarus,' He shouted, 'you can come out now!' He sounded as though Lazarus were a child who was simply hiding in that grave, and now the game was over and it was time for Lazarus to come out for supper. Jesus had a way of saying the most extraordinary things in the most ordinary voice, as though it were all perfectly normal. Listening to Him, I would realize that from the Master's perspective, all His miracles *were* completely normal; they were exactly the way things ought to be, and the rest of the broken world was what was abnormal.

"Anyway, when He told Lazarus to come out of the grave, everything was absolutely still at first; none of us even dared to breathe. And then we heard something, a sort of rustling, shuffling sound, and the hairs on my arms stood straight up.  And the next thing we knew, there was Lazarus in the mouth of the grave, on his feet, all wrapped up in the grave clothes, with his face covered by the head cloth. None of us could move a muscle.

"And then Lazarus broke our spell. 'Let me out!' he said, sounding grumpy and confused.

"Jesus began to laugh. 'Unwrap him and let him go!'

"You see Jesus wanted us to know exactly what His kingdom is like. It's a place where everyone is satisfied; there is plenty of what everyone needs and more than enough to go around. It's a place filled with overflowing joy, where no one is sick or damaged or wounded. Everyone there is whole and complete, exactly what God intended them to be from the beginning of Creation. And when Jesus raised Lazarus, He showed us that on top of all that, His kingdom is a place where death no longer exists. Jesus is God's Son, and the power of His love is even greater than death."

Secret Code:

_____ _____
7-4-2-4   4-1-1-2

_____ _____ _____ _____ _____
6-5-3-3 9-2-6-2 3-3-4-5 1-1-2-4 2-4-1-1

_____ _____ _____ _____ _____ _____ _____
5-1-6-1 8-1-1-2 3-2-5-1 2-3-2-5 7-1-1-4 5-2-9-6 9-3-8-1

10
The Giver of Life

Rachel had a funny feeling inside her. It felt a little like when she was looking forward to something really nice happening, and it was something like the way she felt when her mother held her on her lap, even though Rachel was really too big for that now. But mostly it felt too good to be true, because Rachel had learned that usually the good things you hope for never happen, and almost always bad things happen instead. She frowned, trying to ignore the funny feeling that made her want to smile up at John.

"There's just one problem with everything

you've said," she told the old man in a small, flat voice. "In the end, Jesus' invisible kingdom didn't do Him any good. Because no matter how pretty it all sounds, it doesn't do any of us any good. It's just not real."

Aaron let out a yelp of protest. "How can you say that? After everything Grandfather John has told you? Don't you understand yet?" He shook his head, as though he couldn't believe how slow she was.

Rachel's cheeks flushed. "You can believe whatever makes you happy, Aaron," she said between her teeth. "But I'm too old to waste my time with make-believe."

"But Jesus is real," Aaron said. "Grandfather John saw all these things happen with his own eyes. They're all true."

Rachel shrugged. "So what? Jesus *was* real. He's dead now."

"No, He's not!" Aaron turned to John. "Tell her, Grandfather."

The old man smiled at the two children.

"Remember what Jesus told Martha? He said that *He* is the resurrection and the life. Remember how I told you that Jesus was there when the world was created? Well, that same life that made everything in the beginning is still working now. That same life, that same power will save us from death. Because that life and that power *is* Jesus. And He gives His life to all who give their lives to Him. Even though these bodies will one day die, the eternal part of us will live forever."

Rachel made a face. "Sure. You can believe whatever you want about what happens after we die. No one can contradict you, because except for this Lazarus, no one has ever come back to tell people what happens when we die." She shook her head and folded her arms tight across her chest. "Maybe this Master of yours had some sort of funny power. Maybe He really could turn water into wine and feed thousands of people with just one little boy's lunch. Maybe He could make sick people get better, and maybe He could even bring people back to life again when their bodies were already all stinky and rotten. But, like I said, what good did it do Him? In the end, He couldn't save Himself. In the end, they killed Him. Right?"

"Yes," John said gravely. "They killed Him on a cross outside Jerusalem. Just as we had feared, the Jewish leaders put Him to death. They murdered the giver of all life."

Aaron sat up straight, his eyes shining. "But that's not the end of the story, is it, Grandfather John?" He grinned at Rachel, then turned back to his grandfather. "Tell her what happened next."

Secret Code:

___ ___ ___ ___
1-2-1-1 2-1-8-1 4-2-1-1 1-1-8-2

___ ___ ___ ___ ___
2-3-2-1 4-1-1-2 3-1-5-1 4-2-3-1 2-1-7-6

___ ___
3-1-8-4 1-1-6-3

11

The Resurrection

"I'd be glad to tell her, Aaron," John said. And he began a final story for the children.

"All along, Jesus had been warning us that He was going to die, but I guess we didn't want to hear Him. After all, we believed He was the Messiah—and the Messiah wouldn't die before he got a chance to be king. According to everything we'd always been taught, the Messiah was the person who would win. He'd kill God's enemies with his superhuman power, and then he would set up his kingdom. So when Jesus told us He was planning on dying as part of His mission here on earth, it just didn't make any sense to us. It was one more of those weird things He was always saying, and because we couldn't understand it, we pretty much ignored Him whenever He'd start talking about His death.

"The thing was, though, all along, He had also said that He would rise again. But until it really happened, we just didn't understand what He was trying to tell us. Because this was the most important miracle of all, the one that made sense of all the others.

"So first of all, I guess you need to know that Jesus was really dead. I saw Him nailed up on that cross; I was there, and I saw His blood and His pain. It was the worst day of my life. He was the best friend I had ever had, and I believed He was the Son of God. I just couldn't understand how such a terrible thing could be happening. It seemed like a nightmare. It couldn't be true. Jesus couldn't die.

"But He did. I saw the exact moment when the spirit left His body. His head dropped and

His eyes went blank; He stopped breathing, and we knew life had left Him. A soldier came and stuck a spear in Him. I was an eyewitness to all this.

"Later on, a couple of Jesus' followers who had some money, Joseph of Arimathea and Nicodemus, got permission to take Jesus' body down from the cross. Together, they took the body and buried it in a garden nearby. We all went home, feeling as dark and hopeless as we had ever felt. 'What was the point of everything He taught,' we were saying to each other, 'if in the end He couldn't keep Himself from being killed?'

"Those next couple of nights, I lay awake in the darkness, trying to make sense out of everything that had happened. But I couldn't. I was too sad.

"But early on Sunday morning, Peter and I were trying to choke down some breakfast, when Mary Magdalene came running in, all upset, panting so hard she almost couldn't speak.

She had run all the way from Jesus' grave, it turned out, and when she had caught her breath, she gasped, 'Someone rolled the stone away from His grave!'

" 'What are you talking about?' we asked her.

"She inhaled a deep breath. 'It's true. And whoever did it, must have taken the Lord's body. He's not in the tomb. I don't know where they have put Him!'

"She began to cry, but I was filled with a sudden wild hope. I was remembering another tomb with a rolled back stone, you see, and I was thinking of the way Jesus had laughed with delight when Lazarus came stumbling out of his tomb. So I jumped to my feet, and Peter and I raced to the grave where Joseph and Nicodemus had buried Jesus.

"I have to confess that I beat Peter in the race to get there first—and sure enough, just like Mary had said, someone had rolled the stone away from the mouth of the tomb. I bent over and looked inside. I could see the grave clothes lying where the body should have been, but they were empty. The face cloth was lying to one side, all neatly folded, as though Jesus had gotten up that morning and remembered to make the bed before He went out for the day. Suddenly, I was laughing and crying, all at the same time.

"Then Peter caught up with me and pushed past me. He went inside the grave and looked at the empty grave clothes. I followed him, and we just stood there, staring down at those linen cloths, not daring to say out loud what we were both thinking.

"Finally, we went back home, but we could hardly concentrate on anything. We had that excited feeling in our hearts that something wonderful, something amazing, was about to happen. Or maybe it already *had* happened.

"Later that afternoon, Mary Magdalene stopped by again. Her eyes were shining, and we knew we were right: Something wonderful had happened, something that was better than we had ever imagined.

" 'I've seen Him!' she cried. 'He's alive!'

"I can't describe the joy that swept through me then. We jumped to our feet, demanding that she tell us everything that had happened.

"She had gone back to the grave after Peter and I went home, and she had stood there crying, wondering where Jesus' body had gone. Something made her look inside the grave, just as we had, but this time two angels in white robes were sitting at each end of the place where the body should have been. She nearly jumped out of her skin, but the angels just looked at her, their faces calm and glowing.

" 'Why are you crying?' they asked her.

"She wiped her nose on her sleeve and gulped back her tears. 'Because,' she said, 'someone has taken away my Lord, and I don't know where they've put Him.'

"Before the angels could answer her, though, she saw something out of the corner of her eye. She glanced over her shoulder and saw that someone was standing there behind her. *The gardener,* she thought to herself, too confused from sorrow and fear to make sense out of anything that was happening.

" 'Why are you crying? Who are you looking for?' the man asked.

"Thinking that she was talking to the gardener, she said, 'Please, if you have taken Him, tell me where you've put Him.'

" 'Mary!'

"As soon as He said her name, she recognized Jesus. She let out a yell of excitement. 'You're back! I have You back!'

"He told her gently, 'You can't keep me, though, Mary, not like this. I have to go up to my Father before too long. And I need you to go tell the others that I am alive. Tell them that I will be going up to my Father soon. But remember—My Father is your Father, and My God is your God.'

"So Mary ran and found us and gave us the Lord's message.

"That evening we were all together with the doors locked tight in case the Jewish leaders should find us, and suddenly Jesus was standing there with us. 'Peace to you,' He said, and we heard the joy and love in His voice.

"As He spoke, He held out His hands, so we could see the scars the nails had left in His palms. Then He showed us the place on His side where the soldier had stuck the spear into Him, and we knew for sure that He was really Jesus, our Master. I began to laugh out loud, with tears running down my face. I felt as though I had just woken up from the worst nightmare I had ever had—only to find that a bright and glorious morning had dawned.

"We all gathered around Him. And then He said one of those funny things that took us by surprise again, the way He always did. 'If you forgive anyone's sins,' He said, 'they are forgiven.'

"Peter and I glanced at each other. I was remembering the way I had raced ahead of him that morning, determined to get to the grave first—and I guess he was thinking of the way he had pushed past me to get inside the tomb. We gave each other a couple of sheepish grins, and then we hugged each other. We knew that even something little like that had to be forgiven. We couldn't stand in the presence of our risen Lord knowing that anything was between us.

"The next forty days were wonderful. Now at last we were finally beginning to understand what Jesus had been trying to teach us all along. He wasn't going to set up an earthly kingdom, with thrones and rulers and important people to help the king. Instead, He was the King of a different sort of realm, a kingdom of love and forgiveness that would last forever.

"Still, a few of us kept thinking that He would set up the other sort of kingdom while He was at it. We kept asking Him if now He was going to free our country from the Roman emperor.

" 'God decides when those sort of things will happen,' He told us. 'Don't worry about all that. When the Holy Spirit has come upon you, you will receive power to tell everyone about Me, all over the world.'

"Soon after that, when we were all together one day, Jesus disappeared from our sight—He went up into the sky. Just as He had told Mary Magdalene, He went back to His Father, and we no longer have His physical presence here with us on Earth. But He sent us His Spirit. He is in our hearts now, and nothing ever can separate us from His love. And that is the miracle that happens to each of us."

Secret Code:

———— ———— ————
4-4-8-3 2-1-4-2 9-1-3-2

———— ———— ———— ———— ———— ———— ,
6-1-4-3 7-5-2-1 1-2-6-3 1-1-1-1 3-2-5-6 4-3-5-3

12
"It's a Miracle!"

"Do you understand now?" Aaron asked Rachel.

She sucked in a deep breath, her eyes on John's face. "That really happened?" she asked the old man. "Just the way you said?"

He nodded, and she could read the truth in his gaze. "I saw it all with my own eyes."

Rachel rubbed her eyes with her fists, suddenly as exhausted as if she had worked hard all day, instead of sitting here listening to an old man talk. "I'm not sure," she said slowly, "I'm still not sure I understand."

"No," John said gently, "it is not easy to

grasp the Good News that Jesus brought us. And yet it is very simple. All we have to do is give our lives to Jesus—and in return He gives us Himself, the never-dying Life."

Thoughtfully, Rachel watched an ant crawl across her bare foot. She thought about her father, and how sad she and her mother had been ever since he died. "You really think when we die—when our bodies die, I mean— that we will still be alive with Jesus? Can Jesus really work a miracle like that? Even though we can't see Him?"

John nodded. "One time when Jesus was talking to us, He promised that His Father's house had many different kinds of mansions in it, wonderful homes for everyone, where we can all live forever. 'If it weren't true,' He said, 'I would have told you.' Believe me, Rachel, the Master always spoke the truth. He wouldn't have let us go on believing something if it weren't true. That's why He worked so many miracles. He wanted us to understand the real truth about

His kingdom, a truth that will last forever."

Rachel thought about a wonderful mansion where she could live with her parents in Jesus' kingdom—and then she remembered the small, dark house she shared with her mother. She sighed; she needed to get home and do her chores. Her mother would be coming back soon, tired from her long day gleaning grain. They would have a little wheat to make bread, but her mother would be too hungry to wait, and Rachel had never gotten to the market. She felt tired and sad for a moment, remembering how dark and dreary her life with her mother was since her father had died. But maybe. . . maybe if what the old man said was true, then none of that mattered quite so much. If she were part of Jesus' kingdom, then His love and life were everywhere. Maybe she could even find them in the cramped, dirty house that was her home now. . . .

She got to her feet. "I need to go," she told John. She felt suddenly shy, and she hesitated, wanting to say something more, but not certain how to say it. "Thank you," she said at last, her voice soft and gruff. "Thank you for telling me about Jesus' miracles."

John smiled. "You are welcome, any time.

I like nothing better than to talk about the Master. But wait a moment, child." He pushed himself up from the bench. "Let me get you a basket of food to take home to your mother. I have more than I can ever eat, and it would be a shame for it to go to waste."

Rachel skipped up the narrow street that led to her house, her mind busy. If she gave her life to Jesus, the way the old man had said, would Jesus really fill her with His life and love? Would John turn out to have spoken the truth about Jesus and His miracles?  The basket that hung from her arm distracted her from her thoughts for a moment. It was so heavy that she could hardly wait to show it to her mother. They would have enough food for the entire week, and that in itself seemed like a miracle to her. Now she would have to hurry and do her chores before her mother got back. . . .

When she ducked through the door, though, she found that her mother was already there, sitting slumped on the floor, her face pale in the shadows.

"I'll get busy now, Mother," Rachel said in a rush. "But look what I've brought you." She held out the basket.

Her mother got to her feet, but she ignored the basket of food. She stepped close to Rachel and looked into her face.

"Child," she said slowly, "I can't remember the last time you didn't have a frown on your face." She touched her daughter's cheek with her hand. "But you're smiling!" She took a deep breath and let out a little laugh. "Oh, Rachel. It's a miracle!"

Secret Code:

_____   _____   _____
1-5-4-4   4-1-1-4   2-2-5-3

_____   _____   _____   _____   _____
5-3-4-1   5-1-4-2   1-3-2-1   3-2-3-2   1-4-7-1

_____   _____   _____.
5-2-9-2   1-1-1-2   2-2-2-3